Table of Contents

Monster's Captive

By Luna Jade

COPYRIGHT

MONSTER'S CAPTIVE

Copyright © 2023 by Luna Jade

All rights reserved.

This is a work of fiction. Names, characters, places, and incidents either are the product of the author's imagination or are used fictitiously. Any resemblance to actual persons, living or dead, events, or locales is entirely coincidental.

Published by Beautifully Twisted Publishing
3609 Austing Bluffs Parkway
Colorado Springs, CO 80918
www.beautifullytwistedpublishing.com

Trigger Warning

This book includes depictions of domestic violence and suicide. If these subjects are distressing or triggering for you, please prioritize your well-being and proceed with caution. Consider whether engaging with this content is appropriate for you at this time.

Story Blurb

As a child, I was told that the monster in my closet was just a figment of
my imagination. But one day, he became real and took me away from
my home and family.
I'm trapped in another realm where I will fight for my freedom and life.
But something much more sinister than the monster who took me here
has their sights set on me—they want my head.
I'm the only person who can stop them. I must set aside my fears and
embrace my destiny as a warrior. Because if I don't, no one else will stand
in their way of them ruling this realm with an iron fist.
*Follow Lila into a creepy fantasy world of monsters, dragons, and
other creatures. It's an epic tale full of action, adventure, and
romance.*

Chapter One

SINCE I WAS YOUNG, my parents taught me that the scary monsters in my closet or under my bed were only in my imagination and couldn't hurt me unless I believed in them. They often told me stories about a boy who thought monsters were chasing him from under his bed, but it turned out they were just his toys. However, one day I realized that monsters weren't just make-believe; they existed.

I was in my bedroom in our new house, which seemed forever dark. The silence pervaded the room, aggravated my ears, and made me feel more alone than ever. I could see the night sky through the window and wished I could fly up, following the stars to somewhere more fun. I stood up, walked over to the window, and peered at the starry sky; a sudden calm enraptured me. The vastness of the universe was both humbling and awe-inspiring. I felt small and insignificant but also connected to something much larger than myself. The stars twinkled at me as if they welcomed me into their world. I took a deep breath and smiled. I was no longer alone.

I then heard it.

There was a scratching noise from my closet, so I opened it and pulled back the few dresses hanging there. To my surprise, behind them was a massive, pulsing shape! It was too dark to see, but I knew it was looking at me. Suddenly, the figure moved closer and closer. Then—with a jolt that made my heart jump into my throat—the creature reached out its massive hand and grabbed mine; its ice-cold fingers closed around mine! My eyes widened, and adrenaline shot through every vein in my body as I screamed, which startled my parents into entering the room.

"What's the matter, honey?" My mom asked as my dad looked through the closet.

"I saw a monster!" I shrieked, pointing at the closet. "There was a hand in there!"

My parents looked at me, then back to the closet. My mother put her arm around me, and I wept as she gently rocked me. "There's nothing in there, honey," she said calmly. "It must have been a shadow."

I shook my head. "No!" I said, the tears painting down my cheeks. "I saw a hand! It grabbed mine!"

My mother frowned and looked up at my father, who shrugged, then walked over to the closet and pulled open the door again. He turned on the light, which shone brightly into the dark space—but he insisted there was nothing inside except my clothes, some boxes, and my stuffed animal. "Look, honey. It's just your stuffed bunny, Hops," my dad told me.

I knew better.

I had not been mistaken. There was an enormous creature in my closet, eyes luminescent, as it squirmed around on the floor of the tiny space. Its fleshy body was searching for something—or someone. Still, my parents didn't believe me because they couldn't see it from where they stood. I wasn't sure how they could miss it. The creature was a giant, far more giant than my father. Its eyes were glowing red orbs as it stared at me from behind my parents' backs; then I understood what the thing wanted: me! I wanted to scream, but no sound would come from my throat. I tried to run away, but my legs were frozen in place. Everything happened so fast that it felt like a dream—a nightmare.

They told me to go back to bed because I had been going through some tough things for someone so young. My grandma had just died, and I was constantly picked on at my old school. With my dad getting a new job, we moved to this town—a fresh start for everyone. The move was a lot for me to take in at once, and I felt overwhelmed, especially since I found a monster in my closet the first night; this wasn't the fresh start I was looking for.

Closing the closet door, my parents tucked me back into bed and left the room. And with the sheets covering half my face, my heart was pounding in my chest. My eyes stayed transfixed on the doorknob. I expected it to turn at any moment. And if it did, I would scream bloody murder until my parents came running back in again. I lay there for an eternity, wondering what the monster would do to me if he opened the closet. Every little creak and sound the house made filled me with terror, as I knew the monster could come at any moment.

Nothing happened.

Finally, my heart slowed, and I fell asleep. The closet door was still closed when I woke up the following day. It was time to get ready for school. I was filled with a sense of relief, but I couldn't shake the feeling that I had narrowly escaped something awful. I was too scared to open the closet door to grab one of my dresses from the hook, so instead, I sifted out something from my dirty hamper and sprayed it with a light floral scent. I quickly put my clothes on and hurried toward the door.

"I'm not going anywhere," a creepy voice said.

I froze, my fingers on the doorknob. Then I stood there blinking—was I hearing things? The scratching sounds from last night were coming from the closet! I turned around and saw a shadow creeping toward me. I screamed, but no sound came out of my mouth. The shadow got closer until it was right in front of me. I flung open the bedroom door and raced down the hall to the front door, gasping. I couldn't believe it, but those distinct sounds from my bedroom closet left little doubt. I didn't imagine this. There was a monster living in our house, in my room.

I reached for the front doorknob, but my hands shook so bad that it took me a while to open it.

"No breakfast?" my mom asked from the kitchen.

"No time." Without saying goodbye, I left the house into the breezy morning air. I couldn't breathe until our house was out of sight. My new school was a few blocks down and around the corner. I just hoped the kids there were nicer than the ones at my old school.

I breathed deeply as I approached the school's front gates, and butterflies swirled in my stomach when I stepped into the schoolyard. Everything was different from what I was used to; the building was red brick with tan trim—a far cry from my old school's cream-colored bricks that clashed horribly with bright green grass and orange metal benches. The playground was to the right of the main entrance, and I noticed immediately that many students were standing in small groups, talking and laughing with each other. I felt lonely, realizing I had no friends in my new school. However, I knew that it would be okay. Everyone had to start somewhere and someday I'd make some friends here.

Behind the playground was a dense forest—the thought of it being the same one I'd left behind made me uneasy. I felt like I was being watched, but there were so many trees that it was impossible to see through the forest. The trees were tall, and their branches reached toward each other to form a ceiling. Their movement gave off an eerie feeling, as if something was walking through them—something that made the leaves rustle even though there wasn't any wind.

Chapter Two

THE SCHOOL WAS LOUD and chaotic as students and teachers rushed to their appropriate classrooms. I followed the signs, making my way to the front office. I was told I would have an assistant walk me to my classroom. As I waited, I heard laughter and chatter around me and the ringing of bells that signaled the start of a new school day.

"Good morning, Lila! We are so happy to have you here at Redwood Elementary. Did you find the office okay?" the woman behind the desk asked with a bright smile. She was wearing glasses and a high bun.

"Yes, thank you." I managed to say it despite my nerves clumping into a ball. My previous school's trauma flashed before my eyes—how the girl behind me cut off a chunk of my hair or shoved my head into a toilet filled with urine. I shook my head, releasing the awful things done to me from my mind. A fresh start, I reminded myself. I was starting over and had the chance to make new friends and become part of a new school community. I wanted to believe new opportunities were waiting for me, not just the monster that took up residence inside my closet.

With a deep breath, I took in my new surroundings while I waited for her to finish putting together my welcome packet. I had the opportunity to make a good first impression, and that's precisely what I planned to do.

Finally, she gave me all the paperwork to take home, and I followed her down the vacant hallway. She stopped before a door and said, "This is it. Did you have any questions before I introduce you to your new teacher and classmates?"

I smiled, shook my head, and replied confidently, "No, ma'am."

She matched my smile and said, "Okay, well, let's say hello to everyone."

I swallowed the dry knot in my throat as she opened the classroom door. Immediately, all eyes were on me. I wanted to flee and hide but could only stand there and stare back. It wasn't until my new teacher said, "Hello, Lila, I am Ms. Francis," that I could move from where I was. I took a hesitant breath and tried to smile. The students' gazes followed me as I strolled up to my new teacher. The woman who guided me touched my shoulder and whispered, "Enjoy your new classroom," before quickly disappearing through the door. There was no turning back now. If I fled, the kids would certainly laugh at me, putting a stop to the new start I so desperately needed, but the anxiety was rushing through me as I stood there in front of all my new classmates. I had to inhale an even deeper breath, my nerves tangling together as I half-heartedly told myself I could do this.

"Everyone, this is Lila. She is our new student, so please make her feel welcome."

My cheeks burned as I was introduced, and I attempted to grin as I waved to everyone. Only a couple waved back; the others just stared. I could tell what they were thinking. Because I had anemia, my complexion looked ghostly pale compared to my beautiful blue eyes and black hair. My former classmates called me the devil's offspring. I was accustomed to it, but I couldn't help but worry what people would say if they knew who was beneath the pale skin. Even though I was used to people's judgments, they always bothered me. I just wanted to feel accepted. No matter how hard I tried, I never fit in. I was constantly reminded of my differences, and it felt like I was forever condemned to be an outcast.

"Okay, dear. Find a seat, and we can continue with our reading lesson."

I strolled down the aisle to a desk in the back of the classroom. The girl with the blonde hair opposite me twisted her face at me before returning her gaze to Ms. Francis at the front of the room. As I lowered my gaze to the floor and took my seat, a droplet of sweat fell from my brow. I'd rather be at home with the monster than in this classroom, which was scarier.

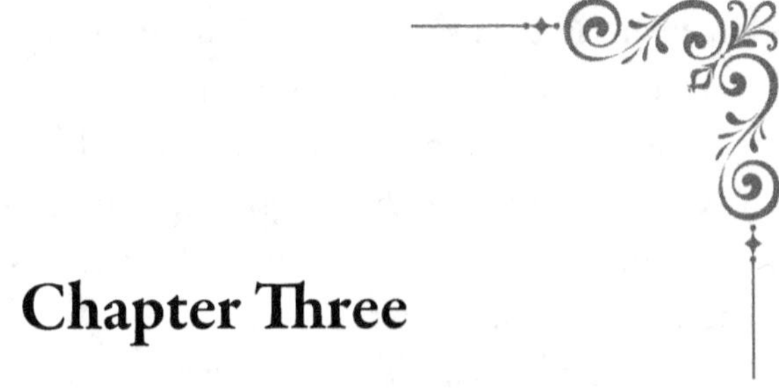

Chapter Three

MY MOTHER HAD TO COME pick me up from school a few hours later because I got into a food fight with the blonde in Ms. Francis' class. She said I started it, which I didn't, but everyone at the table agreed with her, so they had no choice but to send me home.

My father was not going to be pleased. He wasn't as forgiving as my mother. Even so, I was so humiliated by the ordeal that I couldn't look my mother in the eyes as she drove me home. She didn't question me until we were inside the house: "Did you cause that food fight in the cafeteria?" She looked at me with her hand on her hip. I inherited my blue eyes from her, and it wasn't until then that I realized how intimidating blue eyes could be. She'd never looked at me like this before, which made my heart sink to the bottom of my chest.

I had to take a deep breath before I answered, wondering what sort of punishment I was in for even though I didn't start it. She was searching for a reaction in me, but I had no idea what I was supposed to say. "No, I didn't start it. She lied. She kept calling me a weirdo and then threw applesauce at me." The words finally spilled out of my mouth as if they were vomit. I just wanted her to know I did try to be on my best behavior but also had to stick up for myself. I told her she had no right to treat me that way and that expecting me to be something I was not, was unfair.

A pushover.

This was what my dad always referred to my mother as, but then got mad at her when she stood up for herself; it confused me. Growing up in an environment like this made it difficult to know where to draw the line. Applesauce thrown at me was a no-no in my book.

"This will be fun to explain to your dad, Lila."

"Can we just not tell him?" I shrugged my shoulders nervously.

"I will not lie to your father; he will discover what happened eventually. It's a small town."

"I don't understand why you're upset with me. I stood up to her. She was being a bully."

"I am not upset with you. I am upset about the situation. We are trying to give you a fresh start, honey. I just wish you would try harder to fit in."

"Maybe I don't want to fit in."

"That's unfortunate." She inhaled a deep breath. "No matter how much I want to help you, the choice is yours. I know you're a sweet girl with a lot of life inside of you." She got down on one knee before me and tucked a strand of hair behind my ear. I'd always admired my mother's kind demeanor. I only wish my father respected her as much as I did. My father had always been strict, but he was too harsh on my mother. She rarely complained, though it was evident to me that she was unhappy with the lack of appreciation she got from him. Her kindness, patience, and perseverance in adversity inspired me to develop my values.

"Okay, I will try harder."

"That's all I ask, honey. Now, go to your room and think about ways to fix this situation."

No, not my room!

When my mother kissed my forehead, I couldn't argue, so I staggered down the hall to my room. Nothing seemed out of place. I strolled up to my desk and set my bag next to it before lying on my bed and staring at the ceiling, repeating the day's events in my mind. I should have walked away. How much good would that have done? I decided I had made the best choice but told my mother I would try harder the following day. I didn't want our name to be associated with being a problem. As a businessman, my father valued reputation above all else.

I MUST HAVE FALLEN asleep because the next thing I knew, I was jarred awake. Glass breaking. High-pitched screams. Yelling. My heart stammered against my chest. The monster already occupied the only place I felt safe when my parents fought—my closet.

The screams and yells grew louder, and covering my ears did nothing to prevent tears from falling down my face. I knew my dad was upset about me and was blaming my mom for not being more of a disciplinarian like him, and that's why I thought I could act this way and get away with it. I felt like a prisoner in my own home, with no one to turn to for help, and as much as I didn't want to go in the closet, I always felt safer there. I just hoped he would make room for me.

I slowly made my way to the closet, and upon entering, a sense of comfort and familiarity washed over me. It was dark yet vacant, so I slid inside, closed myself in, then pulled my knees to my chest as I tried to drown out the noise. The darkness was almost comforting, and I closed my eyes, praying that the arguing would end.

Then, the heavy breathing started. It wasn't coming from me.

"Leave me alone." I opened my eyes to the darkness, a chill running down my spine as I heard his breathing getting closer to my face.

"From where I see it. I am the only real friend you have," he growled. "Come with me into the dark. I'll keep you safe." His glowing eyes slit into a glare, and they lit up the closet enough that I could see he was extending his claw-like hand to me.

I shuddered, unsure of what to do. I knew I could not trust him, but the way he looked at me made me believe him. "Please, just go," I pleaded, my heart racing and my mind spinning.

His eyes were stone-cold and steely. "One day. You'll see." And he was gone as suddenly as he appeared. Unexpectedly, I found myself frowning as though devastated by his departure. He was a monster, something that evoked fear and danger. But it was my father who terrified me the most. Despite the closet monster's scary appearance, I liked his company.

MY GRANDFATHER CAME to see me later that evening. He and my mother were close, so he didn't mind traveling for the additional hour to see us. His presence was a buffer between my mother and father, who were not speaking to each other. My father pretended to have a Zoom meeting to be excused from the dinner table. *What a relief!* Another day I could avoid my father's wrath.

After dinner, my grandfather put me on the bed beside him and leaned very close, peering into my eyes. "Your mother told me about what happened at school and how you found a monster in your closet. They told you it was all your imagination, right?"

I nodded, unsure where he was going with this. My grandfather was a Vietnam veteran who was blown out of an airplane during the war, and everyone assumed he was dead until he appeared on my grandmother's doorstep. He had been a loose cannon ever since. My mom thought his mood swings were due to his experience in the war. She believed those experiences in Vietnam had shaped the man he was, and his strange behavior resulted from carrying deep-seated trauma since then.

I found his odd personality endearing and never felt judged; I assumed that's why we got along so well.

Two peas in a pod—we shared a mutual understanding of the world, and I found him a good listener.

"Do you think that's true? I don't believe it for a second," he murmured.

I burst out laughing.

He joined in and kissed my forehead before adding, "But don't tell your dad; he'll be furious if he finds out."

"Okay, Grandpa," I said, even though worry had infected me. I could sense darkness deep inside my soul. The monster in my closet was a real, terrifying presence, yet my fascination with it would intensify as I grew older, but I could never bring myself to tell my parents about it again. I would lie in bed each night, desperately hoping to escape the monster's grasp.

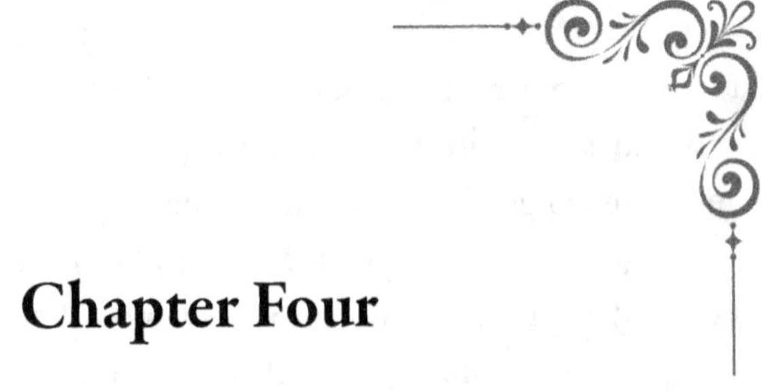

Chapter Four

AFTER SPENDING TIME with the monster in my closet, I had developed a strange attraction toward him. He no longer represented pure evil; instead, he became associated with an exciting romance—a forbidden love between a young girl and an unknown creature. It was as if I was drawn to his mysterious and alluring nature, unable to resist the temptation of exploring the unknown. I found myself yearning for his presence and the thrill of the forbidden love that we shared. It was a feeling that I could not ignore despite the consequences it might bring.

From that day on, my view towards monsters changed forever, and my belief in them would never waver, even if they remained hidden in the dark corners of my mind. Because the monster in my closet wasn't like the hulking ogre you heard about in folklore: he was just massive and strangely irresistible. I got him to promise not to touch me unless he had permission, and he would later cooperate after his many attempts to lead me into the darkness.

I could learn something about him, his weakness.

I hesitated, uncertain of what to do. I had always been warned to avoid the dark, but something inside me began to trust this creature the more we interacted.

As I gazed into his glowing red eyes, a sense of calm washed over me. It was like he could read my mind and understand my innermost thoughts. Despite my initial reservations, I couldn't help but feel drawn to him. Slowly but surely, I began to let my guard down and open myself up to the possibility of a new friendship. I took his hand, feeling his firm grip pull me up. He led me into the darkness, but I wasn't afraid. He had warned me, and I decided to take it seriously. I would venture into the darkness but do it on my terms. I trusted I would be safe, even if something dangerous lurked in the shadows.

My grandfather taught me how to be brave and stand up for what I believed in. I was going into the dark with newfound strength and courage from within, knowing that no matter how scary things got, I was strong enough to take them on. Freedom and hope waited in the depths of this unknown darkness; soon enough, I was ready to face it.

We moved silently until we entered a secret room full of books and candles. He sat in the corner and motioned for me to do the same. He wrapped his leathery wings around himself before finally speaking again.

"This is a place that no one else knows about," he said softly. "It's safe here... I promise."

I stared at him silently for a long time before finally murmuring in agreement, "Okay... thank you."

He nodded solemnly before leaning back against the wall. "I'm always here if you need a friend."

"Is this your home? Where are we exactly?"

And before he could answer, a familiar sound made it to my ears. *No!*

I ran back the way we came, him growling after me to come back. I didn't listen. The way my father was yelling sent a cold shiver up my spine. He was angrier than usual.

I reached the kitchen to find broken dinner plates scattered all over the floor. He then slapped my mother across the face, and I rushed to her aid, only to be shoved aside so he could continue his assault on her. Everything seemed to move slowly, my legs kept giving out beneath me as I tried to get to her and save her. I couldn't help but scream. He hit her so hard she had fallen backward and smashed her head on the edge of the stove. Blood poured from her head as she collided with the ground; she wasn't moving. I ran to her side, still screaming, oblivious of my father still in the middle of the kitchen.

"Momma!" I screamed repeatedly, but she didn't respond. I cradled her head in my lap, not caring that she was bleeding all over me. All I wanted was for her to wake up. Tears streamed down my cheeks as I begged her to open her eyes. I gently shook her and repeated her name, but she still didn't wake up. "Please, Mom." I turned to face my father, who was staring at his hands with his mouth open. "What have you done to Momma?"

He said nothing; he just turned and walked down the hallway. A gunshot rang out throughout the house a few moments later.

I was completely alone now.

My heart rate slowed, and the blood in my veins turned cold. This should never happen to a child. I didn't move until the police officers arrived. They asked me what happened, but I couldn't form the words. Instead, I stood there blinking and motionless until I was whisked to an unknown place. I had to stay there until I was eighteen because my grandfather was deemed unfit to care for me due to his mental issues. When I arrived at the unknown place covered in overgrown vines, I soon discovered it was an orphanage.

I was never adopted.

Chapter Five

YEARS LATER...

For about a year, I had been seeing a therapist to help me cope with witnessing my father kill my mother. I was stunned when my therapist suddenly decided I was untreatable, as the medications were unable to get rid of my hallucinations. It wasn't a hallucination, after all. I'd heard and seen that monster from my closet more frequently lately—but why? Maybe it was because I lived alone now, making me vulnerable to its lure.

He would appear out of nowhere. It didn't matter whether I was out partying or at work; he was always there, as if he was the camera guy and I was the star of a reality show I wanted no part of but had to endure anyway. I would try to ignore the feeling, but he always got what he wanted: my attention for a split-second at a time. He knew that was all he needed to have power over me and control me, especially when I was most vulnerable: sleeping, lingering in my dreams.

During the day, his shadow followed me—a master of deception, convincing me that doing whatever he wanted was in my best interests.

I recognized his presence and felt his eyes on me. His gaze would burn into the back of my neck, sending shivers down my spine. Then I'd hear him breathing and, occasionally, talking to himself or saying my name. I was afraid to turn around and confront him, though I was strangely at ease in his company. I knew I had to face him at some point.

I steeled my nerves and slowly turned. And there he was—not a monster or a figure from my nightmares, but an attractive man, standing in the doorway, his eyes glinting mischievously.

How does he do that? Was he some kind of shifter?

He smiled and said, "Why don't you come to my room? I'll tell you some bedtime stories."

His offer was both inviting and unsettling. I cautiously agreed, and he led me into his room through a dark portal filled with delicate trinkets from a bygone era. We sat at the small table, drank tea as he told me stories of his travels around the world. As the conversation continued, we moved from one topic to another—from history to philosophy to music—and I slowly began to feel at ease. At that moment, I knew I had stumbled upon something special: a chance to meet with someone wise beyond measure who could provide much-needed life advice—all while sipping tea beneath ancient sky-blue wallpaper.

I saw him again several weeks ago while going to the bathroom, and ever since then, after using the toilet and washing my hands, he would stand behind me and whisper things in my ear before disappearing. But then, as I was walking to work one night, he suddenly rushed up behind me, wrapped his strong arms around me, and teleported me back to my apartment.

"You must stay home. It's not safe out there." He yelled.

I was taken aback by his sudden outburst, especially considering his kindness earlier. I found myself struggling to find the right words and feeling frozen to the ground. "Please don't hurt me, I was just going to work." I managed to say.

He then took my hand and put it in his own, and with a sudden quietness, he said, "Forgive me; I was only protecting you." There was such an expression of acute sorrow on his face that I couldn't help but forgive him. But what was he protecting me from?

He handed me a tiny box with a silver trinket inside—a little ship with a heart suspended from its mast—and said softly, "This is for you."

At that moment, I realized this man had seen and experienced more than just this earthly realm. It was hard to find people with such knowledge, compassion, and kindness, so I didn't hesitate to give my deep thanks for the gift of wisdom he had given me through this trinket. Holding the charm between my fingers, looking backward into the past and ahead into the future, I knew it would become a part of me forever.

But what I really wanted to know was his name. I was tired of referring to him as a monster because, over time, he was showing me he was nothing of the sort. At least, that's what I hoped.

"My name is Shal; it means 'peaceful' in Hebrew," he said warmly.

"Shal," I said again, smiling. "Thank you, Shal, for this trinket and the courage to believe in something greater. I apologize for taking so long to come around. I see now that you are not who you seem to be."

"If you let me, I can show you more." His eyes darkened, promising more but also a danger I couldn't quite place. I caressed the charm between my fingers. Shal smiled and reached out to take my hand in his. His words brushed against my ear as he leaned in close. "This charm will aid you in your choice," he said. "It will constantly remind you that there is more out there for you." His words sent a warm feeling through me as I looked into his eyes. They still had a green glow to them. He could tell that my faith in myself was dwindling, so he gave me this charm intending to help me stay strong and never forget that I was capable of anything I set my mind to.

That thought lingered as Shal vanished into the shadows, leaving me to ponder everything he had shown and spoken of. As I returned to the bathroom from the magical portal, I pricked my finger on the trinket's corner, a reminder of how far I'd come and how much farther I still had to go. Tonight wasn't what I expected, but it might have been precisely what I needed as I stood in awe of the mystery of this unfathomable world that seemed so much bigger than myself.

Chapter Six

I HADN'T HEARD FROM or seen Shal in over a week, and I was beginning to think he'd never return. So, to let off some steam, my friends and I dressed up for a masquerade Halloween party at some mountain mansion. Thanks to my friend, who had been fucking the host, a limo arrived to pick us up. The limo wound up a steep hill, eventually reaching an iron gate, which slowly separated to allow us access to the year's biggest party. Everyone would be present at this party. But there was only one face I wanted to see: Shal's.

"What are we waiting for, bitches! Let's go get our sexy masquerade on!" my friend Bridget shouted. She was already drunk from the chardonnay we were sipping on the way here. I rolled my eyes and slid over to get out of the limo. She could be a bit much at times, but she never made me feel less than others and always supported my goals, so I gave her the benefit of the doubt. In the back of my mind, I knew she was doing all this to distract me from the fact that Shal hadn't come around in a while.

As I put my foot out of the limo to hit the street, a hand gripped my arm and tugged me back in.

"What are you doing here?" he said. I gasped, recognizing his voice immediately. I turned to face him, and a smirk ghosted over his lips at my stunned expression.

"Shal! You're here! Where have you been?" I said with a mix of relief and anger bubbling through me. But as he studied me with his glowing eyes through his mask, it felt like all the anger melted away into nothingness, and what remained was my desperate longing for him.

"Who are you talking to?" Bridget asked.

I scrunched my face at her, then glanced in Shal's direction, only to find him gone. I had missed him so much that I was imagining him now. *Great.* My friend was going to think I was a psycho, just like everyone from my past except for my grandfather. He never treated me like I was crazy. My grandfather had been a rock in my life, always understanding and listening to me without judgment.

Inside, the mansion was decorated with all manner of Halloween decorations. I saw a giant coffin filled with candy, severed hands, and some witches brewing their cauldrons on the balcony above. I even saw authentic vampire fangs that could suck blood from a cut on your finger if you weren't careful.

As soon as we entered the ballroom, Bridget's expression changed. She gasped, pointing towards the corner of the room, and I followed her gaze. A tall man with a severe look stood as he stepped forward from the shadows.

When I looked closer, I realized it was Shal.

"Shal!" I said excitedly. He gave me a faint smile and nodded, trying not to draw more attention to him than I already had. "This is Shal," I told Bridget.

She looked at Shal with fear and awe, but he didn't notice or care. His eyes were focused on something else in the room.

Me.

"So, this guy you have been going on about does exist. Nice to meet you, Shal." Bridget said this before leaving to find her billionaire, who was kissing someone else. *That's not going to go over well.*

"Shal, what are you doing here?" I asked.

"I should be asking you that," he replied. "I wouldn't be here for anyone else but you."

I had no idea what to say, so I stood silently. Shal took this as an invitation and kissed me on the cheek. "I missed you," he whispered into my ear.

A million different emotions flooded through me at once. I wanted to admit the same but couldn't bring myself to tell him I'd missed him too. I was torn between wanting to be with Shal and not wanting to get hurt. He was the kind of man who could break your heart without even trying, but I couldn't help but think about what it would be like if he didn't. So, I stepped up to Shal and smiled. He returned the smile, his mask revealing his strong, handsome face along the side, his familiar eyes looking into my soul. His presence filled the room with a sense of security.

As I leaned into his embrace, Shal's scent filled my senses, a unique blend of leather, musk, and confidence that seemed to linger long after he had let go. Breathing deeply, I couldn't help but be enveloped in the moment, feeling a sense of calm wash over me as I savored the sensation of being held so tightly.

"I'm glad you're back," I said softly.

"I'm glad to be back," he replied quietly, his eyes fixed on mine. Everything else faded away as we were the only ones in the room. I looked out, embarrassed by how he made me feel. He wasn't even trying, but I still melted at his touch. It was something about how he looked at me like I was all that mattered in this world. "I've missed you," I finally said, voice trembling. I wanted to take it back as soon as the words left my lips. It would be too easy for him to use them against me.

"You're all I think about," he replied, his voice low and husky. We stared at each other for a moment before I turned away again. I couldn't look at him any longer without wanting to kiss him. My body took over whenever he got near me, and all rational thought flew out the window. I couldn't let that happen. He was dangerous and unpredictable. I had to stay strong and keep my guard around him.

But then, against my better judgment, I looked back up at him. "I can't help it," I said. "It's like you have a pull on me, and I don't know how to resist it."

He was on me again when the words left my lips. His arms wrapped around me tightly, pulling me against his chest so there was no space between us. He leaned close to my face, his lips just centimeters from mine. Our gaze remained fixed on each other, allowing it to transport us away from the world's harsh realities and into our own haven. The only sound in the room was our breathing. There were no words exchanged—just a pure connection. "Thank you for believing in me when no one else did," Shal finally said. He raised my hands to his lips for a soft kiss.

My heart began to race with happiness. It was the most incredible feeling in the world to know that I had found someone who truly accepted me for who I was. What did it matter if he was a monster? He was *my* monster, and he adored me.

Shal pulled me into his arms and kissed me deeply, passionately. I could feel his heart pounding against mine as he pressed against me. I wrapped my arms around him and let myself get lost in the moment, knowing this was right where I belonged—in his arms.

He spun me around the ballroom as a slow song played. His muscular arms held me tight as we danced. His mouth was close to my ear, and I could feel the heat of his breath on my neck. "I want you so much," he whispered. His confession flushed my cheeks, and I was more drawn to him, as he whispered those words in my ear again, "I want you so much it hurts."

I found myself wanting him just as much. I leaned in close to him, my lips almost touching his ear. "Take me away from here," I whispered back.

Over time, we were spinning so fast that everything blurred, and I began to feel the bile rise in my throat. "What's going on?" I asked.

Shal did not respond to my inquiry. The melody that had filled the air moments before had faded away, and I now found myself in an unfamiliar place. Despite this, I was oddly calm. I looked up at Shal, and he beamed back at me. "You are now in a safe haven," he said. "I have brought you into my realm. Welcome home," he added with a warm smile.

Shit! I did say take me away from here, but this was not what I meant! Uneasiness spread through my chest as I realized where I was—somewhere foreign. It was as if I were no longer on Earth.

I looked around me, and my heart plummeted to the pit of my stomach as I realized that volcanic ash covered this place and a distant volcano spewed fire.

The sky was dark and gray, and no plants or trees existed; only mushrooms of all kinds grew here, covering everything in sight.

Shal led me toward a palace off in the distance. I noticed something strange about Shal as we walked toward it—he wasn't human anymore. His wings extended behind him, resembling those of an eagle. However, they were not composed of feathers, but somewhat resembled scales made of leather. I looked up at Shal and saw him looking down at me with his bright green eyes—so familiar it made my heart ache to see them again.

He smiled. "It doesn't matter that I am a monster," Shal said. "You are here with me; this is the only place where we can truly be ourselves." He kissed my forehead softly before twirling me around again, sending me drifting off into blackness again.

HIGH-PITCHED SCREAMS jolted me awake. The curtains were slightly closed, and only the fire in the distance peeked through. I hoped this was just a nightmare and I would wake up any minute. But my heart rate wouldn't slow down, and looking around, I realized I wasn't in my room.

Shal's arms surrounded me, and he pulled me close. His voice was calming and comforting, "We are in the Xul Realm, light years away from Earth. We are safe here. No one can touch us."

My heart felt heavy with despair, but I tried to keep my composure as I looked around again at this foreign environment. Through his embrace, I began to gain a sense of peace. Shal grabbed my hand as we walked into the unknown. Together, we enjoyed a never-ending adventure in this mysterious realm he called Xul.

He whispered, "Welcome to my palace of darkness; nothing but your desire fills this place; I shut the world out—but not you. You will be my one and only obsession."

My heart raced, and a sense of awe and wonder embraced me as my eyes tried to take in all the surrounding beauty.

Finally, I could see the stars in the night sky. They were all different colors, and they twinkled and shone beautifully.

Suddenly, mist surrounded us, appearing out of nowhere, and an unfamiliar spirit lurked. A voice echoed through the darkness, speaking, "Come closer; I will answer your questions." I looked around carefully, wondering where the voice originated from.

Shal encouraged me to step closer, and then it appeared—a beautiful woman shrouded in light. Shal referred to her as Light Xul. She introduced me to Xul's history, and I found out that this realm was actually from another land beyond our wildest imaginations; she told us how long the Xul had been living here and how they were able to manipulate time but would be forever doomed by dark forces if they were to disobey the Gods.

We thanked her for her kind words before traveling farther into his palace. Everywhere we looked, there was beauty and color; I stood in awe as we gazed upon the grandeur. Everywhere I went, I felt the presence of Light Xul following us; each step taken was a journey into a realm of powerful energy.

We even came across creatures unlike anything seen before, from golden unicorns with wings to purple dragons with long tails. Each creature moved gracefully while they contributed to the incredible atmosphere created by Xul's divine protection. As we explored more, I learned more about Shal's story and how he wanted to keep peace and beauty alive.

"You will be happy here with me."

As I took in the breathtaking sight of Xul, I felt torn between its beauty and my responsibilities back on Earth with my grandfather and friends. Although I was captivated, I knew I couldn't stay here forever. So, I mustered up my courage and said, "Shal, I'm sorry, but I can't stay."

I let go of his hand to walk away, but he snatched it back. His nostrils flared, and his eyes were a bright red. He was back in his monster form. "You will never be able to leave. You are mine now."

His voice was low and threatening, and I could feel his warm breath on my skin as he spoke. He led me farther into the darkness, and I sensed Light Xul's absence. I prayed to the gods of the Moon and Sun for assistance and a path out of this nightmare. Though I felt powerless, aware that he'd been plotting this since my childhood, I knew I had to remain resolute if I hoped to flee.

As darkness enveloped me, I shivered from the cold and could only hear my heartbeat thumping in my ears. Despite Shal speaking, his words were muffled and drowned out by the sound of my blood rushing through my veins.

Now, I could feel the hardwood floor beneath me in his bedroom.

The door shut behind me with an ominous click, and I whirled around to face a six-foot-tall man in the darkness. The gaslights flickering on the walls hid his features, and his voice cut through my panic, saying, "You're mine now. Do you understand?"

I nodded, unable to speak.

He moved towards me, and I shrank back into the corner of the room. "Did you hear what I said?" he asked, his voice low and menacing.

I couldn't recall his previous words, but my only concern was my safety. Trembling and feeling lightheaded, memories of his words echoed in my mind, "One day, you'll understand." It dawned on me that he had been preparing me for this moment. Despite my dry throat, I mustered the courage to shout, "I will never belong to you!"

He laughed—a cold sound that made my skin crawl as he moved towards me until my back hit the wall with nowhere left to go. He loomed over me, grabbing my hair and pulling me up to face him. "MINE," he repeated. His body squashed me into the corner. He smelled like ash and fire, and his red eyes were piercing, but he was the only thing in focus in my vision.

I tried to scream, but my throat wouldn't work. It was like he had cast some sort of paralysis spell on me—I couldn't make a sound. I grew increasingly panicked with each attempt; finally, "please" came out as barely a whisper.

He leaned down and put a hand on either side of my head, pinning me against the wall. His face came closer until our lips touched, his breath hot on my cheek. I didn't know whether to be relieved or terrified. He pulled away slightly, leaving only an inch between us. Then he walked away, his face beet red, all while gritting his teeth. He turned back to me as if to say something else before disappearing into thin air. I was shaking from head to toe from the adrenaline of being so close to him, so close to this enigmatic man—this monster.

I sighed, getting accustomed to my surroundings. The room had a bed, dresser, and two doors. One of the doors was firmly shut; the other door, however, had been cautiously cracked open, revealing a shroud of darkness that kept its secrets hidden. Only a tiny amount of what lay beyond could be seen through the narrow opening.

I uncovered a pair of chairs on opposite walls, creating an intriguing symmetry. A small desk was also hidden in another corner of the room, along with an old lamp, weathered by time, adding a touch of vintage charm to the scene.

The room's centerpiece is the bed, draped with a thick quilt that envelops the space in a cozy atmosphere. The dresser and desk, both substantial and made of solid wood, stand as sentinels, offering ample storage space with their numerous drawers.

An open window lets light filter in, delicately dancing through the gauzy curtains. These curtains create an ethereal ambiance, making the air feel almost fragile as if every breath carries a certain weight.

While being a prisoner in another realm may not be ideal, there was a silver lining to be found in this room.

But the revelation of never being able to go home had the bed calling my name. I lay on the bed, the mattress a fluffy cloud, swallowing me, and within the next blink, I was fast asleep.

I SWALLOWED HARD, REALIZING I wasn't in the bed alone. I reached over to touch him on his muscular stomach. His hand found mine quickly, lacing our fingers together as he pulled me close to his chest. "Good morning, beautiful," he said with a sleepy smile as I melted into his warmth, trying to calm myself down by inhaling his scent until he kissed me gently on the forehead. He kept his arm around me as we lay there in the morning sunlight, relishing the warmth of each other's embrace. "I can be your greatest fantasy or your worst nightmare. Your choice," he said, sending both chills and heat down my spine. He continued, letting me know everything would be all right if I followed his rules and didn't try to escape.

I felt a sense of comfort knowing this place might not be so bad, but I did miss my grandfather, and he was bound to notice I was missing any day now. But for the time being, I would try to be on my best behavior until I could devise a plan to escape. I hugged Shal tightly and whispered, "I choose fantasy; thank you very much."

His laughter ricocheted off me, rattling my bones. "I am as much a prisoner in this realm as you." He said this, smiling softly. Then he took my hand and guided me towards the window, where we watched the volcano erupt together.

"What do you mean?"

"You will understand soon enough." He smiled again. We stood there in awe as the bright orange lava cascaded down the mountainside, illuminating the sky. Shal then sighed and turned away. "When I was a child, the gods casted a spell on this realm, preventing us from escaping and only allowing us to visit other realms for a limited time."

I stumbled backward, shocked, to hear that he had been cursed and trapped here since childhood. My heart dropped to the bottom of my chest, thinking how lonely Shal had been all this time and had chosen to spend his time with me, deemed an outcast, when he could have taken any girl he wanted.

"Lila?" His bright eyes dulled a shade, pulling me into him.

I kissed him on the chest and said, "No more loneliness." A comforting sentiment. He won't be alone anymore. However, armed with this knowledge, it would complicate my escape plan.

I couldn't leave him trapped here.

He hugged me tightly and thanked me. We stood there for a while, staring at the lava, before heading off to explore more of this strange realm. Despite our differences, we both knew one thing for sure: in our hearts, we were no longer prisoners in this realm—at that moment, I was beginning to feel free in his arms. He gently brushed a strand of hair away from my face and kissed me on the forehead. He knew what I was thinking but wasn't angry; he was simply resigned to his fate. "Let's make the most of our time here then," he said with a smile, and I couldn't help but feel strangely grateful for the opportunity to share such a moment with him.

"Have you ever ridden a dragon before?"

The thought of riding a dragon had never crossed my mind. I scrunched my face at him. "Seriously, dragons only exist in movies and video games back on Earth." I laughed. "Yesterday was the first time I saw a real-life dragon."

"Even better. I want to give you many *first* experiences," Shal said, winking. There was no secret that I was still a virgin. I mean, he had been stalking me in the shadows for years. My heart was pounding, but I felt strangely at ease. "Let's do it!" he said with a gentle smile, holding out his hand.

Despite my fear, I couldn't ignore the thrill in my chest as I gasped and turned away. I cautiously approached him and placed my hand in his, feeling an overwhelming sense of bravery and excitement inside me. Looking up at him, I saw trust and understanding in his eyes, and a surge of courage filled my body. This monster had a playful and gentle side, acknowledging my fear yet welcoming my touch.

We walked hand in hand, venturing deep into the unknown until the palace seemed to disappear entirely, and the sky above had turned from a bright red to an inky black. I usually would have been filled with fear, but what surprised me was that I wasn't scared. I was safe with Shal. His hand on mine was warm and reassuring.

We eventually came to a grassy cliff edge, looking out into the valley of the dragons below us. The sight took my breath away. Hundreds of majestic creatures scattered across the hills, each one more majestic than the last. Shal explained that riding one required slow introductions because these were some of the oldest dragons who had lived here since before other creatures or beings ever set foot there. They were like walking history books, able to tell stories of all the people who came before us.

Shal led me down a path through the valley toward one of his favorite dragons, a beautiful creature with emerald scales named Keliath. As we walked, Shal told me that the dragons were the most important beings in this valley. The gods had created them at the beginning of time and given guardianship over Xul. They were almighty and all-knowing but also very kind and loving. They helped Shal whenever needed and taught him many things about how this valley worked.

He gestured for me to step forward, and without thinking twice, I did so, taking off my shoes and feeling the soft grass beneath my feet for the first time. I waved hello to a few other dragons flying by as Shal explained their unique traits, outlining which breed each one belonged to and what kind of temperament they had. Shal was right; the valley was magnificent. I saw mountains in the distance and a lake to my right, but they were dwarfed by the sheer size of those dragons flying overhead. I couldn't help but be amazed at how majestic they looked as they flew through the air, their wings flapping with ease and grace as they soared above us. I noticed that the dragons had a hierarchy. There were larger, more powerful dragons with large wingspans flying high above us while smaller ones flitted below them. The bigger dragons would occasionally swoop down and snatch up one of the smaller dragons in their talons before flying back up into the sky.

I turned to look at my captor and saw that he was smiling at me. "What?" I said, looking back up at the dragons flying overhead.

"You look like a child again," he said. "It is rare to see humans so entranced by our world. It has been many years since I have seen someone react this way to seeing dragons interact for the first time."

I looked away from the dragons. "I'm sorry," I said. "It's just that I didn't know dragons were real until yesterday. And then when I saw them flying overhead, well... it's just amazing."

Amazing? That's the best you can come up with?

"Don't be sorry. I'm glad you think so."

After we said goodbye to our dragon friends, it felt like an eternity before we finally started heading back toward his palace on the dark side of the realm. As I walked through Silvio's village with Shal, there was a noticeable difference in him: something that wasn't there before I saw those magnificent dragons with him. He smiled whenever anybody caught his eye, giving them a respectful bow as he passed by their doorsteps—it was almost hard to believe this was still the same monster who had held me against the wall yesterday. I couldn't help but wonder what had changed him so much. I was excited to discover Shal's more gentle side and spend time with him. Each experience with him seemed to surpass the previous one. Although he was quite intimidating yesterday, today, he revealed a completely different aspect of his personality—as if the dragons we encountered had stirred something within him.

I wanted to know more about his past and how he had become this monster. He had been brooding but today, he seemed as if he didn't have a care in the world; there was a spring in his step and an air of confidence around him that was almost contagious. It felt like I could do anything when Shal was around; he made everything seem possible—even things like changing dragons into humans or back again.

Chapter Seven

BACK AT THE PALACE, the staff served us an unusual dinner of things I didn't recognize, and I swear my meat was moving on my plate. But Shal insisted it was delicious, and I didn't want to look a gift horse in the mouth. After dinner, we retired to Shal's chambers. He told me he wanted to show me something and walked over to a hidden panel in one of the walls. He pulled on it, and it slid open, revealing a room full of books!

As a child, books were my comfort, and I thought it was sweet he had remembered this after all this time. "I know how much you love reading. I thought these might help pass the time."

"Thank you, Shal. They're wonderful!" I said, rushing over to the shelves and running my fingers across their spines. There were books on every subject, from history to science, even magic. There was even a small collection of books written by Shal himself. I looked at him, surprised. "You wrote these?" I asked.

He nodded. "Yes, I did."

"Why didn't you tell me?" Shal was becoming sexier to me by the second, and he was already fucking sexy as hell.

"I didn't think you'd be interested in reading my books."

"You're wrong," I said. "I'm very interested in reading your work. Would you tell me a bedtime story?" I wiggled my eyebrows at him.

Shal's eyes widened at my request. "You want me to tell you a bedtime story?"

"Yes, please. It's been so long since anyone has read to me."

With a bob of his Adam's apple, he grabbed me by the hand and led me to the loveseat. I sat beside him, and he took a deep breath before opening the book. For a monster, he had beautiful penmanship. I listened to him read and couldn't help but smile. I used to love hearing my father read me stories before bed as a child. Shal's voice was deep but not gravelly or scratchy sounding; it was smooth and soothing. It reminded me of the sound of honey pouring onto freshly baked bread.

Shal continued reading. "She was a woman with so much fire inside her that she could burn the entire world with one glance. There was no one who could match her beauty or strength. She was more than a woman; she was a goddess. But sometimes it was as if she didn't recognize her own power..."

My cheeks heated at the words he had just read aloud.

He looked at me and smiled. "Do you like it?"

I nodded my head slowly as if in a trance.

"I wrote it for you."

I couldn't believe what I was hearing, and yet, at the same time, it made so much sense. Shal was always telling me how beautiful and powerful I was, but somehow, I just never believed him. Now, hearing his words and seeing the look in his eyes as he read it to me made me believe. He looked at me with such reverence and love, I knew he wasn't lying. My heart began to beat faster as I thought about how he had shown me how much he cared for me over the years. Shal had always been there for me, although he came off as a stalker at times, now I knew why. He was the one I could count on to be my rock and support me through anything.

I closed the book and set it to the side as I straddled him. I caressed his surprisingly smooth face. "I am sorry it took me so long to see you. You're not a monster, Shal; you're the sweetest, most thoughtful being I've ever known." He smiled and leaned in to kiss me. I could feel his hot breath on my lips before our mouths met, and I savored the moment. His tongue slid into mine, caressing it tenderly as if he were kissing me for the very first time. Shal pulled back after several moments and looked deep into my eyes with such passion that I felt like we were one being, sharing the same soul, heart, and mind.

"Since the first moment I saw you in your room, Lila. All I ever wanted to do was protect you. I never meant to scare you."

I smiled back at him, holding his gaze for a moment before I took his hand and led him to the bed. We lay down together, and he wrapped his naked body tightly around mine as if he were afraid I might disappear if he let go. Shal kissed me again, softly this time, like we were sharing an intimate secret between us while the rest of the world fell away into oblivion. I was falling for him, acutely aware of Shal's every touch against my skin and how his body molded perfectly to mine like they were made for each other.

Our mouths found each other repeatedly as if they were magnets drawing together from opposite ends of the universe. Shal's hands moved up and down my back, grabbing my ass; he could not get enough of me. I ran my fingers through his hair, feeling the silky curls against my palms. His kisses grew more intense, almost desperate with need as if he had been waiting for this moment all his life.

When we finally broke apart, we were panting like we had run a marathon. I smiled at Shal, and he looked back at me with an expression I had never seen before on his face, but one that was unmistakable in its meaning: love. Shal looked down at me, his eyes seeming to search my face. "I love you," he said quietly. "I know it may take a while to love me back, but you are my everything. You are mine forever."

Tears sprang to my eyes, a mixture of joy and worry. I didn't want to stay here forever. I missed my life back home. But I also knew I was falling for Shal. I wanted to find a way to make this work.

Shal had his arms around me and was pulling me close to him. He looked into my eyes and smiled as if he could read my mind. "I know this isn't the life you wanted, but it's what I want for us."

I looked down, avoiding his gaze. "I know."

"Don't worry, I'll take care of everything." He kissed my forehead, sealing his reassurance.

"But my grandfather. He depends on me to take care of him. He must be worried sick. Can I please go—"

He jumped up from the bed, nostrils flaring. "I thought I made myself clear. You are mine forever!"

I looked up at him, eyes wide. "Please, Shal! I must go home! My grandfather is sick and needs me."

He raised his fists in the air. "NO!"

I stood up and backed away from him. "Please, Shal. He's all I have."

He lowered his fists and stared at me silently for a few minutes. Then he walked over to the window and opened it wide. "I'm not enough for you? Do I not please you?"

I shook my head. "No! It's not that. I love being with you, Shal."

He looked at me sadly. "Then why do you want to leave?" I walked over to him and put my arms around his waist. "I don't want to leave because I'm unhappy here. But you can't whisk me away and expect me to forget my old life and the people I care about."

He sighed, turning to rest his chin on my head. "I know, Lila. But I want you all to myself."

I looked up at him and smiled. "You *have* me."

He didn't return my smile. "And I will keep you whether you like it or not." Suddenly Shal vanished into thin air, leaving me to cry by the window, longing for my old life.

I LAY AWAKE THAT NIGHT, thinking about what I should do. Should I stay here and be with the man I was falling for? Or should I run away and try to find a way back to my world?

When the door creaked open, my heart skipped a beat when Shal walked inside. He sat next to me on my bed and held me close with one arm while stroking my hair with his free hand. "I know you're scared," he whispered. "But we're going to be okay."

"Can I at least check on him?" I asked. "I just want to make sure he's okay."

Shal was silent for a moment before he spoke. "You can go see him, but only for a minute." I nodded and got up from bed, following him outside into the hallway. A dark portal appeared, and we stepped through it, arriving outside my grandfather's house. I saw him through the window sitting in his favorite recliner with a shot glass of liquor in his hand.

My grandfather was many things, but he was not a drinker.

My heart clenched because I knew why he was drinking—he hadn't heard from me. I knocked on the door, and he looked up. He set down his glass and stood up, walking over to the door. He opened it slowly, and we stared at each other for a long moment. Then he opened the door wider so that I could come inside. When I did, he wrapped me in a hug, which made me cry harder than before.

"Child, where have you been? I've been worried sick."

I glanced over my shoulder to look at Shal, who was still standing where I had left him, but now he was wearing a black suit and tie; he was warning me with his eyes that I didn't have much time. "Grandpa, I am okay. I just wanted to let you know I am checking myself back into the ward, and I am not allowed to have visitors or outside phone calls."

He let go to look at me with concerned eyes. "I'm not sure I want you at a place like that, honey. How am I supposed to make sure you're doing all right?"

"I am not sure either, but I have to do this. Shal came with me to make sure I got there safely."

My grandpa turned around and looked at him. "Shal?" He reached out his hand to shake Shal's. "Nice to meet you."

"Likewise," Shal said before stepping back out into the darkness.

My grandpa looked like he wanted to say more but refrained. "I guess if that's what you want, then you have my support, but promise me you will call me as soon as you can."

I nodded and gave my grandpa a big hug goodbye. "I will. I love you."

"I love you too, honey."

I turned around and walked out into the darkness where Shal was waiting for me. The tears streamed down my face because, in my heart, I knew this was the last time I would ever see my grandfather. Him closing the door behind me was as if he was closing it right over my heart.

"Come on," Shal said as he started walking toward the portal.

I took a deep breath and followed him. "Wait." I stopped in my tracks.

"What?" Shal turned to face me with a look of concern. "I thought we had an agreement?"

My knees gave way, and I sank to the ground on all fours. Bile rose in my throat. "I don't know if I can do this. I can't just leave him alone with no one to care for him. It's not fair, Shal. Please don't make me do this. *Please.*"

Shal's face softened, and he walked over to me. He touched my shoulder. "I know this is hard for you, but we have no choice."

With anger building in my chest, I shot up from the ground. "*You* don't have a choice, but *I* do." I shoved my hands into his chest, but he didn't budge.

"No, you don't," Shal said. "I'm sorry, but this is the only way." He grappled me around the wrist and pulled me toward the portal as I kicked and screamed.

The portal was a swirling mass of colors now. It looked like a tornado as it picked up speed. Still, it was only big enough for Shal and me to fit through.

As we drew nearer to the darkness, a sense of foreboding washed over me. The swirling colors enveloped us, tugging at my body like a straw, pulling liquid. My limbs felt like they were stretching like rubber, and everything was happening too quickly for me to catch my breath. I was at a loss for what to do. But Shal led me through the portal just before it closed behind us.

We were now back in his bedroom. The last place I wanted to be. "I *hate* you!" I screamed.

Shal turned to me, his eyes red. "I know. And I'm sorry."

"That's not good enough," I said as I tried to push past him.

He grabbed my arms and held me back. "It's all I can give you." He let go of me and walked over to his bed, where he sat. I stood there momentarily, unsure what to do or say. Then I sat down next to him. Shal turned and looked at me with his big eyes, now their hypnotic shade of green. "I'm sorry," he said again.

"Why is it all that you can give me?" I asked him.

"Now that you have been here, the same rules bind you. I don't know if you've noticed in the past, but I was only able to see you for a moment. The masquerade party was pushing my luck."

"I noticed," I said. "And it hurt my feelings."

Shal looked away from me as he spoke. "It was painful for me as well."

"What happens if you were to not abide by the rules of this realm?"

"That answer is simple. You *die*."

I looked at Shal and tried to read his face, but it was blank. Shal looked down at the ground. "I am sorry, but there is nothing more I can do for you or anyone else in the realm of Xul."

"The gods make the rules?" I asked. "And why haven't you or anyone else ever challenged those ridiculous rules?"

Shal looked up at me with a sadness that made me take a hard gulp. "I did that once," he said, lowering his head between his shoulders and hugging himself in response. "It cost me everything." He looked so defeated—what had he lost? His family? Walking through the village the other day, I noticed that no one else resembled Shal. Like he was the only one of his kind.

The village people had pale skin. The women had long black hair that hung past their waist and deep brown eyes, while the men had white hair that was shaved close to their heads. Their clothes were colorful but simple: a tunic and pants made from cotton or linen with leather boots on their feet. Shal explained that they used to be much more advanced than they are now—their technology was beyond what Earth has today.

They once had flying cars and buildings that were made of glass. They could cure any disease or illness, but they lost it all during the war. Shal told me that he didn't know who started the war or why it happened, but he said a lot of blood was spilled on both sides.

"That's horrible. I had no idea."

"I know," Shal said. "It was a very sad time in our history." Shal told me that he'd been alive for about a hundred years, and he was a child when the war took place. He said his memories of it were foggy and incomplete, but he remembered trying to protect his family and was cursed for challenging the gods' rules.

"I don't understand," I said. "What do you mean?"

Shal told me he was a human before, but he became something else entirely when he was cursed. He said that his body began to change and no longer looked human. His skin turned black and leathery like a lizard's, his eyes turned bright red, and his teeth grew sharp enough to slice through bone. He said he felt like he was being poisoned from the inside out like he was slowly dying. He told me that the gods were punishing him for choosing to defy their rules and protect his family from their wrath."

Those bastards! I had no idea what they looked like, but they were on my shit list. Can't you get rid of the curse?" I asked.

"No, the gods sealed it, and they are the only ones who can break it," he said. "I have to live with this curse for the rest of my life, and there's nothing I can do about it."

My heart ached for him, knowing how deeply he had been hurt. It made sense that he didn't want to be alone; I wanted us both to be free of this place—but how?

Chapter Eight

I SOUGHT OUT THE DRAGON with emerald scales named Keliath because I remembered Shal saying dragons were like walking history books. I was hoping to find information on the gods that could help me, even lead me to some method of destroying them.

As I entered the dragon valley, friendly roars greeted me from overhead. Smaller dragons slithered up and licked my arms. I noticed Keliath was perched on a boulder too small for him and was amazed at how gracefully he balanced himself. Keliath's scales were a deep emerald green, and his eyes were silver. He had large bat-like wings folded neatly against his back, and I could tell he was strong even though he didn't look intimidating. He looked at me as if he knew exactly why I was there.

"Keliath," I said happily.

He smiled and nodded, then hopped off the boulder. He folded his wings out and flapped them once before resting them against his back again. "Lila, it's a pleasure to see you again. What brings you to the valley without Shal?" he asked with a deep voice that sounded like it was coming from the bottom of a well.

"Honestly, I don't have a lot of time. I asked him about the gods, and he kept changing the subject. I was hoping you could give me some insight?"

Keliath sighed and looked off into the distance. He was silent for several minutes before he spoke again. "What is it that you want to know? Opening up old wounds is difficult for Shal." Keliath paused, breathing smoke out through his nostrils, his silver eyes dulling a shade. "It was a devastating time in Xul history when the war happened."

"What caused the war?"

Keliath closed his eyes, the smoke still streaming out of his nostrils. "I am sure Shal mentioned the village as an advanced people. So advanced it was beginning to make the gods uncomfortable, so they enforced rules to control them. Most of the village fell in line, but there was a group of people who resisted, including Shal's family. His father led the war."

I brought my hands to my mouth. "Oh, my."

Keliath nodded, his eyes still closed. "Shal's father was a strong leader who led the people well. They fought hard but eventually lost most of their men in battle." He opened his silver eyes again and looked at me, letting out another cloud of smoke.

"Lila," I heard a familiar voice say from behind me. I knew he would notice I was missing from the palace sooner rather than later. I was just hoping for more time. *The story was getting to the good part.* I turned around to see my Shal standing there. He had a stern expression as he looked between Keliath and me.

"I was just telling your Lila more about the village," Keliath said with a smile.

"I see," Shal said, looking at me. "And did she enjoy the story?" Shal was no fool. He knew I was up to something.

I took a deep breath and let it out slowly. "It was very interesting," I said, sounding as innocent as possible.

Shal narrowed his eyes at me and stepped closer. He put one hand on my shoulder and squeezed gently until I looked at his face. "I know you're up to something, Lila," he said softly, looking down at me with concern.

"I just want to figure out a way to help you."

"I don't need any help," he growled before stomping back to the palace, motioning for me to follow.

Keliath's wings drooped as he nodded in Shal's direction. "Go take care of our dark prince. I'll be here whenever you want to learn more."

"Thanks, Kel," I said, giving him a smile before running after Shal. "Wait up," I called out as we reached the palace doors.

He didn't slow down or even turn around to acknowledge me but kept walking inside and up to his room without saying anything else. I sighed and followed him all the way there, where he slammed the door closed behind us. I stood there for a moment, playing with my sleeves. I didn't know what to expect from him and wasn't sure if I should leave. The room was dark except for a lamp on the desk, but it was light enough to see that Shal's face was flushed red with anger. He turned around to glare at me. "What were you really doing down there in the valley?"

I blinked, surprised by the question. "What do you mean?"

"Don't play stupid. I know you were probing Kel for info about the gods." His voice was low and dangerous.

"I was just wondering what he knew about them," I said.

"And?" Shal's eyes narrowed.

"And nothing, that's all."

He stepped closer to me and curled his fingers around my chin, tilting my head up so that I looked directly into his eyes. "You're lying."

"Shal, I swear—"

"It doesn't matter," he interrupted. "I know what you're up to." He released my chin and stepped back. "Planning an attack on the gods to escape is a death sentence. Trust me, I've tried."

I stared at him, speechless.

Shal sighed and ran a hand through his hair. "The gods are too powerful," he said. "It doesn't matter how many of us there are or what we have in mind—they always win."

I was still staring at him, my mouth hanging open.

Shal shook his head and laughed softly. "Don't look so shocked," he said. "It's not as if you thought I didn't know what you were planning." He turned away from me and started walking down the hall.

I stood there for a moment, my mind whirling. My heart was thumping in my chest, and I felt light-headed. Then I ran after him.

"Shal!" I shouted. My voice echoed down the hall, and I winced at how loud it sounded in this place.

Shal stopped and turned around slowly, his eyes narrowing. "What?" he asked.

I took a breath, trying to calm myself. "What do you mean you know what I'm planning?" I asked.

Shal snorted. He started walking again, this time more quickly—almost running down the hall and away from me. "I know everything," he called over his shoulder as he went. "You're not nearly as clever as you think."

Wow, powerful goddess and all went out the window real fast.

I stared after him, shocked into silence. I felt like someone had just punched me in the stomach and knocked all the air out of me. *Does he know? How does he know?* I followed Shal down the hall. He reached a set of double doors and pushed through them without slowing down. I ran forward, following him into the main courtyard, where he stopped and turned around to face me again.

"Just like you want to make me happy, I want to do the same for you. For us. As much as you say we are safe here. We are only safe if we follow the gods' rules, right? The people and creatures of Xul deserve better, and you know that. Your father, he knew it too," I said, holding back my tears.

Shal looked at me momentarily, like he was trying to decide whether he should answer my question. "I have seen what happens when people make their own rules," he said finally. "I have seen it time and time again. They are always served a terrible fate. I don't want that for you."

I shook my head. "You are wrong, Shal. You are not seeing things clearly. Your father wanted to help his people; that's why he broke the rules in the first place."

"No," Shal said, looking away from me again.

"My father is the reason I was served this fate."

"What do you mean?"

Shal looked back at me and sighed. "My father was a good man, but he was also arrogant and selfish. He thought that because he had been chosen by the gods to lead our people, meant he could do whatever he wanted. He even cheated on my mother."

"That's terrible," I said. "I'm sorry."

Shal nodded, then continued. "It's all coming back to me now. The gods were not happy with my father's behavior, and they punished him by making my mother barren, making me an only child. She was devastated."

"Oh, no." I pulled my hand to my chest.

"My father was also distraught but refused to admit his mistake. So, he started a war with the gods instead, and as much as we resented my father for what he had done, my mother and I stood by him. The village stood beside him. People died, including my parents, and I became this...*this* monster."

I wedged my body between his strong thighs, lifting his chin so his eyes met mine. "Look at me. You are not a monster. You are the most hypnotizingly attractive being I have ever met, and you are stronger than *any* god." I could see the doubt in his eyes, so I continued. "I know you are strong because I feel it when we touch. You give me strength and keep me safe." I squeezed his hand, and he smiled. "Besides, you have a lot to live for. You have me now, and I need you. Xul needs you."

I pulled him to his feet, and he wrapped me in a hug. "I need you too." He kissed me softly on the lips and then held me at arm's length. "But how do I know you aren't just trying to save yourself? How do I know this isn't just some elaborate plan to leave me behind?"

"Because the more I get to know you, the more in love with you I become." Shal and I had so much in common, which made me think that the universe brought us together for a reason. "We can't let the past control us. We have to live in the now and make our own future." I was hoping that he would understand what I meant by that. "I want to make a life with you, Shal. Will you give our future, Xul's future, a chance?"

"Okay," he said, smiling and nodding. "Yes, of course, I will—I love you so much that I'd move Heaven and Hell for you if it were what you wanted, but at the same time, I don't want anything bad to happen to you."

"I know. But we must try. Let's give Xul its freedom back."

"I'm so happy," Shal said, leaning forward and kissing me. I knew he was worried about what would happen if we tried to free Xul. But the idea of not even trying was even worse than facing the consequences later down the road. "I hope that you're right about this because I don't know the first thing about leading people into war."

A thought occurred to me, and I started grinning. "I know the perfect person for the job."

Chapter Nine

MY GRANDFATHER'S EXPERIENCE as a Vietnam vet makes him an excellent source to guide us into this war with the gods. He has a vast knowledge of the subject, and he will be able to help us understand how we might survive in it—this world that is so different from our own.

How could I tell my grandfather the truth, though? He wasn't one to judge, but even this was out of the box for him. And it was still hard for me to wrap my head around this realm and what it contained: gods; dragons—creatures!

And when I did tell my grandfather the truth, I wasn't sure if he would believe me. He was a man of science and logic—not fantasy. And even if he did believe me, what then? What would we do once we had this knowledge?

I decided I couldn't tell my grandfather. Not yet. It was too much to take in all at once. I needed time to process it independently and ask Kel more questions about the gods before I came to him with this craziness.

This time, Shal accompanied me to the valley, groaning. I appreciated his willingness to try, but it didn't come without him complaining.

Kel was perched on his usual spot, and he gasped when he saw Shal trailing behind me. He smiled, showing off his sharp teeth as we greeted him. "Good morning! You're early today," said Kel.

"I'm sorry, I couldn't sleep last night, so I figured I might as well come down here."

Kel's smile faded, and he frowned. "What is it? What happened?"

I took a deep breath before spilling the tea. I whispered so only he could hear me. "We want freedom for Xul."

Kel's eyes widened, and his jaw fell open. "What? You can't be serious! What about the village?"

The words tumbled out of my mouth before I could stop them: "I know it's dangerous, but I don't care anymore. It's time for us to change things around here."

"Lila, I know you are new around here and still learning your way, but the gods are nothing to mess with. Shal, I know you've told her."

Shal nodded. "I have, but she doesn't seem to understand how dangerous this could be."

Kel looked at me with a stern expression and said, "Lila, I know you want to help the people of Xul but freeing them will only bring more trouble than good."

I don't know if it was because I was picked on my entire life that made me immune to this, but I couldn't tolerate injustice. Something had to be done. I gritted my teeth and shook my head. "No, it won't! If we all work together to free them then they can live their own lives again."

Kel sighed and said, "Lila, you don't understand. The gods are not just beings who live in the skies above us. They are everywhere, they see everything that happens in the realm. It would be nearly impossible to get an upper hand."

Shal nodded in agreement. "If this is what you want, you're going to have to live with the fact that people and creatures will die before freedom becomes our reality."

I knew this would not be an easy task, but I felt in my heart that it was the right thing to do. "I'll do whatever it takes, even if it means sacrificing myself," I said with a determined look on my face.

Shal grabbed my arm and spun me around to face him. "Absolutely not."

"But I'm willing to die for this cause," I pleaded. "For you."

Shal shook his head and said, "If you die, all of your efforts will have been in vain. There is a way to stop them without fighting hand-to-hand, but it requires an incredible amount of power."

"What do you mean?" I asked.

"We can use Xul's powers to stop them," Shal said.

"But how?"

Kel chimed in, blowing smoke out of his mouth. "But that would cause Xul to collapse, and no one knows what would happen to this realm and everyone in it after that. We all could still die an excruciating death. Now, you know why we haven't attempted an escape."

"But what if we could find a way to stop them without using Xul's powers?" I asked.

Shal smiled, "I love your optimism. That would be amazing. Maybe there is another way, but I'm afraid no one in Xul knows what it is."

"You said Xul was once an advanced village, right? Maybe not all has been lost, maybe some evidence of their technology is buried or hidden somewhere, and we can recreate it to destroy the gods."

Kel and Shal nodded in agreement. "There are no records of Xul that survived the war; everything was burned and destroyed. However," Kel said, "I might know a dragon who might help us, but he isn't exactly the friendliest dragon around. Also, he lives in the most dangerous part of Xul, closer to the gods. It's impossible to get there without being killed by one of their creatures."

Freaking great. My head started spinning with regret, but it was too late to turn back now. "No matter how dangerous the place may be, we have to try," I said.

"Then that's what we will do," Shal said. "Kel, get a reliable team together. We fly at dawn." Shal walked off with his head held high, and his chest puffed out.

I looked at Kel and couldn't help but smile. Shal was a brave and powerful being, and he just needed a little reminder.

"I don't know what you did, Lila, but keep it up." Kel winked at me before taking off into the sky with a woosh that knocked me to the ground. I laughed at myself and went to search for Shal. I was a little worried about what he would say, but I knew that if anything went wrong on this mission, it would be my fault, and I didn't know if I could live with the guilt.

I was surprised at how easy it was to find Shal. He was waiting for me outside of the palace and looked a little nervous when he saw me walking towards him with a smile on my face. "I'm sorry if I offended you earlier, Lila. I didn't mean to be harsh, but sometimes when people get too relaxed, they are more likely to be careless."

"Don't worry about it." I put my hand on his shoulder and looked into his eyes so he knew he could trust me. "I'm just glad that you're taking me on this mission. I know it will be hard, but I'm confident we can do it. Because we have the dark prince guiding us." I shoved him with my shoulder as I sat down next to him.

"I hate being called that." He smiled at me, and his face seemed to relax slightly more. "I was worried you would feel uncomfortable around me after our conversation with Kel."

"I do feel uncomfortable, but it's not because of you," I said. "It's because I'm worried about our mission." He nodded, and we sat there in silence for a moment. "I'm glad that you want to do this with me. It sounds stupid, but I don't want to do this without you."

He shook his head, smile growing wide. "You don't have to worry about that. We're in this together no matter what."

"I know," I said. "It's just hard to believe that we're doing this." I looked up at him. "I mean, how could anyone think that this is a good idea?" I giggled.

He chuckled at my response. "You're something else, you know that?" he said, pulling me close for a kiss. Our tongues met, and I moaned as his hand wound through my hair to hold me closer. He squeezed my ass and lifted me into the air, carrying me down the hall. I wrapped my legs around him and he pushed open the bedroom door then kicked it shut behind us. We fell onto his bed together and he pulled my shirt off over my head. "I love seeing you like this," he said as he ran his hands over my breasts. "My innocent beauty."

I giggled, and he leaned over to kiss me again. His fingers found their way under the waistband of my pants, and he pulled them down, revealing my pink lace panties. He moaned when he saw what I was wearing and pushed me onto my back so he could slowly peel the panties from my body. My heart raced as I awaited my first of many experiences.

Chapter Ten

SHAL'S WARM HANDS MOVED up my thighs and over my stomach until they reached my breasts, and he carefully cupped each one in his palms, exploring and caressing them as he looked into my eyes filled with longing and adoration. My body responded to his touch, quivering with anticipation as he teased me, bringing my body to a state of pleasure I had never experienced before. "Oh, don't stop, Shal. I love feeling your hands on me."

"Oh, don't you worry; I don't intend on stopping anytime soon. You have no idea how long I've been waiting for this moment to finally claim you as mine." He pulled me to the edge of the bed, forcing my legs apart. He blew hot air all over my sensitive skin, sending a shiver of pleasure up my spine. He was already an expert in making my body respond to him.

His lips found their way up my legs and stomach, grazing against my soft skin. "The smell of your skin drives me crazy." I could feel the heat emanating from his body, and my heart raced faster and faster with each brush of his lips. "Delicious," he said as his lips moved down to my center, lashing my swollen bud with his tongue.

"Oh, Shal. I want more," I pleaded, my body arching off the bed.

His reply was an unspoken agreement as he spread my legs wider, giving himself greater access to my pussy. And without hesitating, he tasted me, sucking and licking, making me scream at the top of my lungs. His technique was exquisite, as if he knew my body better than I did. He explored every sensitive spot, as if he were reading a map that only he could interpret. His touches were gentle and firm, exploring my innermost depths, and sending me into a frenzy as I desperately tried to control my body from shaking. His expert caresses ignited my passion, and I felt as if the flames of his desire were consuming me until I spilled over the edge with a moan. His mastery of my body was unparalleled, and I was left in a state of bliss.

He crept up my body, leaving a trail of kisses, before sucking my hardened nipple into his mouth. I wiggled under his weight as he pinned me to the bed with his massive body. His tongue tantalized me as he moved further up my body, joining our lips together as his cock stabbed into me.

"Please, I want you inside me, Shal." He moved slowly and gently, pushing deeper with each stroke until he was fully sheathed in me. I moaned in pleasure and delight, my entire body buzzing with the sensation of his cock filling me. Our bodies entwined and moved together as if we had done this a thousand times before. We moved faster and faster, both of us on the brink of orgasm.

"Shal!" Sweat dripped down our faces, our breathing becoming heavier as we moved together.

"That's it, Lila. Tell me you're mine. Tell me you belong to me."

"Shal. I am yours. From the moment I first saw you again in my apartment, my heart belonged to you. It just took me a while to realize what you already knew."

In response, he growled, thrusting himself into me at a dizzying pace as the bed rocked underneath us and the headboard dented the wall. His deep voice rumbled with a possessive force as he said, "Yes, you are mine." His words opened a secret floodgate of desire in me, and my body seemed to awaken with an undeniable intensity. I screamed as my release came hard and fast, leaving me breathless and weak. His intensity shook me to my core, and I realized that, despite how much I had thought I knew about myself, my heart had been missing something for a long time. It had been missing him.

"I'm coming," he roared as he lifted his head back, his eyes glowing that menacing shade of red. His expression mirrored mine, and I could feel his muscles tense as he pushed himself further into me, spilling his seed into me and filling me to the brim as it leaked out and ran down my legs. He fell on top of me, panting. I held him close, allowing his heart rate to regulate.

It was the first time I'd ever felt so connected with someone, and it made me feel like I could survive anything. Even a war against the almighty gods everyone in Xul kept harping on about.

He rolled off me, and I watched him as he stared up at the ceiling. "You know...I hope you won't become too clingy after this."

I pushed him, laughing. "Don't flatter yourself."

He rolled onto his side, wrapping an arm around me. "This was what I'd always dreamed of, holding you like this." He murmured into my ear.

"This does feel nice being with you like this," I said.

Soon, his sweet nothings lulled us both into a deep sleep.

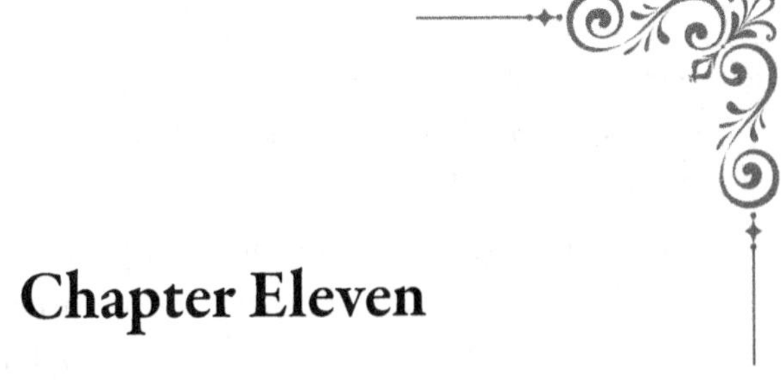

Chapter Eleven

I DON'T KNOW WHAT WOKE me up. It was still dark outside, and I could tell from the lack of sound that even his guards were asleep. There was a rustling in the bushes outside his window, though—just a small one, barely enough to make noise. So, without waking him, I snuck outside to investigate, when something jumped out of the shadows and grabbed me around the neck with both hands.

"What the fuck?" I cried, but it was too late—the creature had a firm grip on me and was dragging me down the palace steps. I tumbled all the way down to the bottom before realizing what happened. Then, my assailant pulled a knife from his belt and held it against my throat. He had dark skin, dark hair, and eyes staring right into mine with such intensity that I felt like they were boring holes into my head. "What do you want?" I asked, trembling in fear.

"Shut up!" he hissed at me. "You don't speak unless spoken to! Now get on your hands and knees, like the dog you are!"

"She is not a dog," a voice erupted from behind us, and I knew it was Shal coming to my aid. He stomped down the palace steps, causing them to crack as he was in full monster form, and I scrambled to my feet away from the both of them.

The creature with the knife turned to face Shal and gave him a dark smile. "Oh, if it isn't our dark prince coming to the rescue," he said, his voice dripping with sarcasm.

"I am the protector of Xul," Shal said proudly as he stepped closer to me.

"Yes, yes, we all know that you are the protector of Xul, but what is she to you?" he asked.

"She is my mate," Shal said with an evil grin.

"Oh really? And how do I know that she wants to be your mate?" he asked as he turned his attention back to me.

I stood there and looked at the two monsters in front of me. The one with the knife seemed to be taunting Shal, but why? And what did he want from me? I had seen him before somewhere, but I couldn't remember where.

"I know that you have been stalking us for some time now," Shal said as he stepped closer to the creature with the knife.

Then it dawned on me. The Halloween masquerade party. He had been so focused on something when I first saw him in the ballroom, but I assumed it was me.

"You can't have her. She's mine!" Shal yelled as he lunged at the other creature. They fell to the ground and rolled around momentarily before Shal could pin him down. The other creature struggled; Shal was too strong for him. He pulled back his fist and punched the creature in the face, letting out a loud groan as he did so. "You tell the gods if they want a war, they've got one."

The other creature laughed, which only enraged Shal more. He punched the creature repeatedly until he let out a final groan and fell limp beneath him.

Shal let out a sigh and stood up, looking over at me. "Are you okay?"

I nodded, not sure what to say. I couldn't believe my luck when he came out of nowhere and saved me from that vicious creature; but I couldn't figure out why he was after me in the first place. My heart was still pounding as I looked up at him, grateful for his help.

Shal helped me brush the dirt off me. "Let's get back inside before any more of those creatures show up." He turned around and began walking back toward the palace, leaving me no choice but to follow him.

"What was that thing?" I asked as we made it back to his bedroom. The guards were now in full force around the palace.

That was a Drakon," Shal said as he sat down on his bed. "They are creatures that live in the mountains and come down only when necessary."

I looked up at him, my eyes wide with fear. "You mean to tell me there's more of those things?"

Shal's face grew cold as he looked at me. "Yes," he said, his voice low. "There are many more Drakons that roam this realm." I was left speechless as he spoke about their ruthless and dangerous nature. "They are loyal servants to the gods," Shal continued. "That's why Kel said they had eyes everywhere. The Drakons are always watching. And that one seems to have taken an interest in you."

"That's what you were so focused on at the masquerade party. Was he following me then?"

Shal let out a winded breath. "Yes, I think he has been following you for a while. That night I teleported you home. I was protecting you from him. He was stalking behind you and probably had nothing but the worst intentions in mind. Sorry I didn't tell you sooner. You were already going through a lot, and I didn't want to alarm you. All I could do was protect you then."

I shook my head. "Why does he want me? I'm nobody."

Shal laughed and leaned back onto the bed. "You don't see it yet, but you are quite the hot commodity around these parts—so much so, the gods are sending Drakons to warn us."

"Are you serious?"

Shal nodded and sat up again. "Very much so. A Drakon is a very rare sight and when they show up in our realm it means something big is coming."

"So, the gods know my plan already and are pissed."

"Yep—"

"Stop right there! Yes, I know you told me so, and I'm an idiot, blah, blah, blah." I started pacing back and forth. I was furious with myself and the gods for getting me into this mess. I had no clue what I was going to do next or how I was going to get out of it. But whatever it was, we needed to act quickly.

"So, what do we do now?"

Shal shrugged. "I don't know. I guess we will wait until dawn and deal with it."

"*Ha! Ha!* You're not helping," I said as I sat down on the bed again.

"I'm sorry, I don't know what else to say. We're stuck in this together. No one ever said defeating a god was easy."

I muttered under my breath. I sighed, ran a hand through my hair, and stared at the blank wall in front of me. "This sucks."

"I don't know why, but the gods wouldn't send a Drakon unless they were concerned," he said. "I hadn't seen one during the war my father led—which means...maybe you're on to something! Maybe we do have a chance." He gave me a bear hug. "You are my powerful goddess, and you are going to save Xul."

A wave of energy surged through me. It was nice to have someone who believed I could change the world.

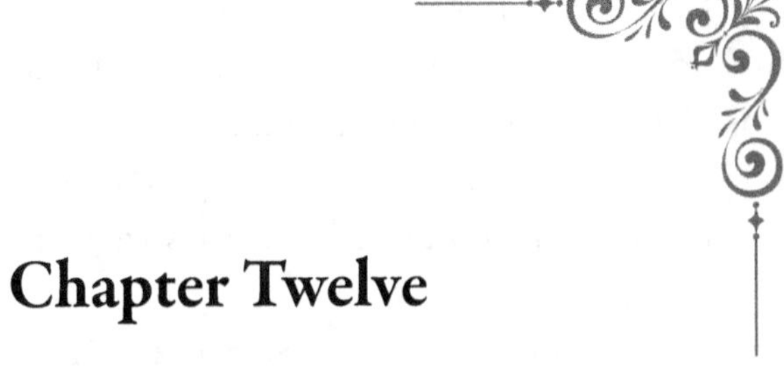

Chapter Twelve

KELIATH GATHERED A team of dragons to assist us in flying over the most dangerous part of Xul. He told me this was referred to as the "land of the dead" because Alzres was a zombie dragon who resided there. He trusted my judgment that we should attempt such an audacious plan—but he wasn't about to let me go solo. I wasn't sure whether he was checking up on me or whether he wanted to make sure I didn't get into too much trouble. Whatever the reason, it was an honor that he trusted me enough to send his best men with us. It also made my heart swell with pride when I saw how beautiful they were—like a dream come true. The dragons were indeed the most beautiful creatures I had ever seen. Their scales were iridescent and shone like a thousand jewels. They had long, curved necks that arched gracefully above their massive bodies, giving them an almost regal appearance. And their eyes—as big as my head—were green with gold flecks throughout like tiny stars in a night sky.

Then it dawned on me. *What a minute.* "Did you just say...zombie dragon?" I was terrified of making the wrong decision and putting the lives of Keliath's dragons, Shal, and everyone else in this realm in danger. I knew that if we made the wrong decision, I would never forgive myself for putting everyone through this. The weight of this responsibility was pressing down on me, and I began to doubt my own judgment and abilities.

"Indeed, a zombie dragon," Keliath said. I couldn't tell if he was amused by my surprise or simply being polite; either way, his expression looked quite draconic at that moment.

I let out a low whistle. "Is he going to try to eat us?"

"He might if you upset him; that's why I mentioned he is not the friendliest."

"Fucking fantastic. We are flying over the most dangerous part of Xul to ask a zombie dragon for help and pray he doesn't have us for breakfast. Way to go, Lila," I said, mentally kicking myself because I had to be a hero and save the realm from the gods.

Keliath held out a claw, and I took it. "You're going to have to hold on; this is going to be a bumpy ride."

"Are you sure?" I asked, looking down at the drop below us.

Shal kissed me on the cheek. "You're going to do fantastic things." He then slapped me on the ass, and the sting spread heat all over my backside. "Now, get on your dragon and be the leader I know you can be." He winked before leaping onto a black dragon with red eyes that vaguely resembled him in his full monster form.

Shal's encouragement and challenge had me clambering onto Keliath's back, ready to embark on the adventure ahead. I knew this was my chance to prove myself and become the hero I had always dreamed of being.

With a sense of determination, my heart racing, I wrapped my arms tightly around Keliath's neck, feeling his powerful wings beat against the inky sky. I could hear the rest of the team of dragons and village volunteers following behind us, their roars and shouts spurring us on. As we flew closer to the erupting volcano on the other side of the realm, sweat dripped down my face from the heat. The intensity of the moment was palpable, but I refused to back down. Together, we would face whatever lay ahead with courage and strength.

As we approached the mountain, my dread deepened when I took in its creepy appearance and saw bones scattered across the land below it.

"I've changed my mind," I said, tightening my grip around Kel's neck. "I don't want to meet this zombie dragon anymore."

Kel's chuckle vibrated my entire body. "I'm not sure that's an option," Keliath said. "We've come all this way, and we're almost there." He flapped his wings faster, and we sped up to a dizzying speed. I closed my eyes and held on tighter as we raced toward the mountain of death.

I couldn't believe what we were seeing. It was something out of a horror movie, but much, much worse. This was where horror movies went to die. The scene was so gruesome that I had to look away. It was as if every nightmare I ever had was coming to life right before my eyes. I felt sick to my stomach and couldn't shake the feeling of dread that had settled over me. I knew that I would never forget this moment, no matter how hard I tried. It was like a scar on my memory, and I knew that I would carry it with me for the rest of my life.

We are dead meat!

A long winding valley led up to the mountain, and along its path were bones of every kind, from animals and humans alike. They were strewn everywhere like a macabre carpet that stretched for miles.

Keliath banked left and circled around the mountain as far as we could go before we reached a sheer rock face that cut off any further progress. He landed on a ledge just below it and turned his head toward me. "We're here," he said simply and nodded toward the mountain.

I had witnessed many horrific events. I knew that this was something different, something worse than death. The air was heavy with the smell of decay and the sound of dying things crying in pain echoed against the rocks. The mountain loomed over us like a giant sentinel, unmoving and unblinking. I shuddered at its solemn presence and looked up at Keliath for an explanation.

"We are on the mountain's peak," he said, "the very top." He turned his head away from me as if to say, 'no more talking'.

"What is it?" I asked softly but urgently, fearing something terrible would happen. Keliath didn't reply, he just turned back toward the mountain and stomped a heavy foot against the ground. I turned around just in time to see something emerge from the rock.

It was a big, black, and terrifying zombie dragon! He let out a mighty roar that billowed into clouds of green smoke, and his eyes glowed with fire.

My heart stopped and my legs weakened as he flew over us. Panic set in as I realized that the dragon had seen me. I tried to stand up straight, but it was too late. Keliath had to remind me to stay calm. The dragon circled around again and landed on the mountain peak next to me.

"Hello," he said in a deep voice that echoed all around us, "I have been waiting for you, Lila."

"Me?" I spoke. "But why? You don't know me." Right then Shal and the others flew over the mountain and landed behind us, keeping their distance. We wanted Alzres to know we meant business, but we didn't want to piss him off either.

"I know all about you," said the dragon, "and I have been waiting for you to come here so that we could meet."

"But why?" I said again, feeling like an idiot. This zombie dragon was intimidating and scary and I was forgetting how to speak English. *Boy, is he impressed...*

"Because," said the dragon, "you are the one who will free me from this mountain." I couldn't believe what I was hearing. His dark eyes were fixed on me, and I felt like he could see right through me. His words sent shivers down my spine, but I couldn't bring myself to move. Alzres lifted his head and roared, and I was sure that he would burn me to a crisp if I didn't do as he said. So, I nodded my head in agreement.

"I will free you from this mountain," I said, and it sounded like the words were coming out of someone else's mouth.

The zombie dragon smiled at me then, and his smile almost made him look kinder—almost human. "I knew you would," he said. "You are the one."

Alzres approached me and gently touched my arm with his wing. The texture was surprisingly soft, considering it was made of scales. His gaze was intense, and I found it difficult to break eye contact.

"Please," I said, my voice was barely above a whisper. "Tell me what you want from me. What do I need to do?"

Alzres laughed then, but it wasn't mean or cruel—it sounded like he was just happy to be alive. Well, as alive as a zombie dragon could be. "You already know," he said. "I want you to free this realm from the gods."

I swallowed hard. "How?"

"Each god rules with their own magic over their own part of Xul. If we break their bonds to their lands, all the magic will be released into them, and they will explode. The gods themselves will not survive this—not even their most powerful ones."

"But what about the people?" I asked. "What about everyone else?"

Alzres' expression turned into a frown as he lowered his gaze towards his feet. After a moment of thoughtful silence, he finally spoke up. "To be honest, I'm not entirely sure. It's hard to say whether they'll make it or not."

I looked back at Kel, Shal, and the others, unsure of what to do. It seemed that no matter what I did, lives would be lost, including those of innocent people. I didn't want them to die. The people of Xul had already endured so much suffering. What would be the point of all their pain if they were just going to die anyway?

But to my surprise the volunteering villagers who came on this trip cheered, chanting, "freedom," on an endless loop. And I knew if they were willing to fight then so were we.

"What do we need to break the gods' hold from each land?" I asked.

"Blood," Shal said.

"Ah, yes," Alzres said. "The gods need to be returned to their full power. A blood sacrifice would be required by all the lands before they could be restored. The only way is to drain someone of great power in each land who has been chosen by the gods as their vessel for this purpose—someone who has been given a gift from them, giving them greater strength than others.

I gasped, pointing at Shal. "But–but you were chosen. You are someone with great power."

He shook his head. "I wasn't chosen by the gods, but the people. I wasn't willing to be used as a tool for them."

"Then who?"

"Light Xul," Keliath said.

"You mean, we have to drain blood from that sweet woman? How much blood?"

"As much as we can," Alzres said. "And then, when the land is restored, we must use that blood to restore order and balance."

I looked at him in horror. "You want us to kill her? How can that be?"

Keliath sighed. "She has to die so that the land can live again."

"I hate this."

Shal came over to me. "I know this isn't the news you wanted to hear, but in order to achieve freedom, some sacrifices must be made. Light Xul has existed for centuries. If you can persuade her, I believe she will support the idea." Shal's words made me think. I was the one in the way of Xul and their freedom, and I didn't want to be that person any longer. I realized then that for Xul to be free, I would have to make a difficult decision. But was I ready?

Chapter Thirteen

AFTER DAYS SPENT PREPARING for war with the gods, and convincing powerful beings in each land to sacrifice their blood to us—including Light Xul—we were ready. Mentally, I was not, knowing I had to sacrifice a sweet woman who harbored so much light; her smile never wavered whenever we spoke, and she was as cheerful as ever. Had she come to terms with her fate?

"My dear." Her glowing hand brushed over my shoulder. "What is on your mind?"

I bit my lip. "I wish there was another way. You don't deserve this."

"I understand," she said softly, leading me to the garden where we could escape the curious gazes of the villagers. We stood surrounded by colorful mushrooms and the calmness of nature. "I have had a long and wonderful life. It gives me comfort to know that Xul will benefit from my sacrifice. You don't have to worry, my dear. I am grateful to you for your bravery and for showing that this was the right decision. You have made Shal and everyone very proud."

As we talked, I couldn't help but feel a sense of calm wash over me. It was amazing how just having her by my side made all the difference. With her support and encouragement, I knew that we could overcome any obstacle that came our way. Together, we made a great team.

Then within the same breath, a swarm of Drakons emerged, determined to undermine our progress. However, we had anticipated this and were well-equipped to handle the situation. Thanks to our preparation, their efforts were unsuccessful. Throughout it all, I was grateful for the steadfast presence and support of Light Xul. Her unwavering commitment to our shared goals was like a shining light during the darkness.

Despite facing the wrath of the gods, we stood our ground and refused to let them take away our freedom. Our leader, Shal, commanded our army with unwavering confidence, and I was grateful to be fighting alongside him. Together, we made an unbeatable team. With a solid plan in place, there was no way we could lose. Our army, composed of a diverse group of creatures from different lands, had the advantage of strength and power. The gods may have relied on magic and their warriors, but we had something even greater—a fighting spirit that could not be broken.

We had another important member on our team. Although I was hesitant, I eventually confided in my grandfather about our peculiar situation. To my surprise, he was completely supportive. During our journey through the portal last night, he seemed unaffected until we reached Xul. At that point, he experienced intense nausea and dizziness. Nevertheless, he was eager to explore Xul and all it had to offer.

"I'm starting to see why you love that old man so much," Shal said.

"He's a riot, isn't he?" We both laughed watching my grandfather ride a dragon for the first time. It was a good feeling. It was like everything was right with the world, and nothing could stop us. I knew that we were going to win this war, and I also knew that I would never have to worry about being lonely again. Because I had the two men, I adored the most beside me.

"Taking a dragon into battle is so much cooler than an airplane," my grandpa shouted.

"Just wait until we get to the battlefield," Shal replied. "You'll see just how much cooler this is!"

"Giddy up, dragon! Let's show these gods they've messed with the wrong grandbaby."

I could tell that Shal was excited, and I knew that he wanted to show off to my grandpa. So, when we got close enough to the battlefield, he made the dragon go into a steep dive. It was beautiful. The sun was shining down on us, and all around us were thousands of soldiers fighting for their lives against an army of god warriors. I had never seen anything like it before. It was a beautiful, terrible sight to behold. I could feel Kel's power surging through me as we moved toward the ground.

The ground rushed up at us and I could feel Kel's wings flapping behind me. Then, Shal pulled on the reins of the dragon, and we stopped in mid-air. It was incredible! I looked back at my grandfather, and he had a huge smile on his face.

"What?" I asked, smiling back at him.

"I was just thinking how proud your mother would be of you right now. Standing up for what you believe in."

I looked at him with a raised eyebrow and he laughed. "Don't get me wrong, I'm proud of you too!" he said as he patted my back. "I just don't want you to forget that your mother wanted this for you."

"Thanks, grandpa," I said as I smiled at him. "I won't forget." I turned back to find a god warrior shooting at us.

"Dive!" I screamed, pulling on the reins, and signaling Kel to fly down to the ground. I had no idea what was going on, but I knew that if we didn't get out of there, we were dead. "This way!" Everyone on their dragons followed behind me and Kel as we flew off to the left and around to the back of the gods' castle. I looked over my shoulder to check on everyone and saw that they were all okay. I breathed a sigh of relief and turned back around, only to see another god's warrior shooting at us from the balcony. "Shit!" I swore as he hit Kel in the chest with an electric arrow. Keliath roared in pain and lurched forward, sending me falling off his back. I hit the ground hard and rolled several times before stopping at a tree.

"Lila!" I heard Shal scream behind me as he flew down to my side.

I turned to look at him and saw that Kel was struggling to stay afloat; he was losing altitude fast. "Shal," I said as I tried to stand up, but my legs wouldn't work properly.

"Stay down, Lila," he ordered as he landed beside me. "The gods will kill you if they see you."

"No! I won't let them kill him." With all my strength, I ran full force, ignoring the pain shooting up my legs and aimed my gun at the warrior."

"Don't shoot, Lila," Shal shouted, attempting to grasp my arm to prevent me from acting. However, I had already launched several rounds at the warrior, leaving him incapacitated. While I noticed the warrior falling, there was no time to celebrate as Shal's voice echoed in my ears once more. "Run, Lila," he commanded, pivoting towards the other warriors descending upon us. Despite my attempt to escape, I was seized by the hair and hurled to the ground. The last thing I recollect is Shal calling out my name before everything went dark.

AS I OPENED MY EYES, the first sensation that hit me was the throbbing pain in my legs. Suddenly, I heard a voice calling out my name. I looked up to find Shal and my grandpa kneeling beside me. It was then that Shal broke the news to me. "I'm sorry," he said, as he caressed my cheek, "Kel didn't make it." My heart sank with the weight of those words, and a scream ripped from my throat; all I saw was red in my vision as I jumped to my feet, adrenaline fueling my veins.

I lashed out at the warriors who were standing around me. Shal tried to hold me back, but I was too strong. I grabbed one of them by the neck and threw him across the courtyard. His head cracked against the wall with a thud. *Holy shit! How did I do that?!*

The other warriors started running away as they saw this, but it didn't matter because I had already killed three of them by then. I don't know where this newfound power came from, but I wasn't going to let it go to waste. The gods and all their warriors were going to die today. Keliath's death was going to mean something.

Seeing my anger, Shal, and my grandfather, along with the rest of my team, followed suit. They started attacking the warriors with their abilities I could feel my power growing within me with every kill we made. The gods didn't stand a chance against us because we were too fast for them to keep up. Another roar sounded from the sky; a green smoke fog rolled in. The smell of death and decay followed. I turned around to see our zombie dragon friend, Alzres. He had opened his maw—releasing a cloud of toxic gases into the air.

The fog spread rapidly, like a blanket of death. The warriors became ill, their skin turning pale and their eyes bloodshot. Some of their eyeballs popped out of their skulls and fell to the ground when they inhaled the poisonous mist. The fog rolled over the battlefield, and it made me feel even stronger. I could hear the gods coughing and gagging above as they tried to breathe through the poison. They didn't have much longer before they were dead.

The fog became a thick, black cloud that had no end. It was filled with a foul-smelling gas that made it difficult to breathe. The warriors who were caught in the fog around us began vomiting, bleeding from their eyes and noses.

The gods were not immune to the fog either. They tried to fly away, but the fog was too thick. They were forced to land on the ground, where they were quickly overcome by the poison. They coughed and gagged, and their skin turned pale. Their eyes rolled back in their heads, and they fell to the ground.

I watched as the fog consumed the battlefield. The warriors and the gods alike were no match for its deadly power. Soon, the entire battlefield was covered in a thick blanket of fog. The only sound was the wind blowing through the trees.

"Thank you," I mouthed to Alzres as his large black body flew over us to unleash more death. Alzres smiled at me and nodded his head. I could see the gods starting to recover, they were slowly getting back up on their feet and fighting again. The fog was still thick on the ground, but it was beginning to clear up as Alzres flew higher into the air. He soared around in circles above us, letting out another cloud of poison that made the gods cough violently once again.

Shal saw this as our opportunity to set our plan in motion. We signaled for my grandfather to alert the sacrifices to get in a position to perform the ritual. As the ritual began, we moved in and attacked. The gods were confused by our attack, but they quickly realized what was going on. It was a blood bath from there on out.

"Run!" Shal shouted. "They're going to explode. Run, get as far away as you can. You don't want to be near them when they do."

As I ran, I heard thundering explosions behind me. I turned around to see the world around me being consumed by a massive firestorm. The gods were gone, but their magic was still alive and well. Even as I ran for my life, I could feel the heat from behind me. I knew it was only a matter of time before it would consume me. The flames were getting closer and closer, and I knew I had to do something. I looked around desperately for a place to hide, but there was nowhere to go. The fire was all around me, and I was trapped. I closed my eyes and waited for the end.

Suddenly, I felt a cool breeze on my face. I opened my eyes and saw that I was standing in a field of green grass. The fire was gone, and the sun was shining brightly. I looked around in confusion, not sure what had happened. Then I heard a voice.

"You are safe now," the voice said.

I turned around and saw a man standing in front of me. He was tall and handsome, with long flowing white hair and a beard. He was wearing a white robe, and he had a kind smile on his face. I was taken aback by his appearance, and I couldn't help but stare at him.

"Who are you?" I asked, finally finding my voice.

"An old friend," he said, smiling.

That voice. I was at a loss for words. I simply stared at him, the smile on his face unmistakably Kel's. It seemed impossible, but there he was, in human form. However, before I could even begin to ask him how or why he was there, he suddenly disappeared into thin air.

DAYS LATER...

As I sat upon the very boulder where Kel once rested, my sorrowful tears flowed ceaselessly down my face. His life had been lost in the valiant fight for our freedom and I couldn't help but feel responsible for his untimely demise. However, I couldn't disregard the potent energy that coursed through my veins, never fading in intensity, turning my hair purple. The more I pondered on it, the more I hoped that it was Kel's magical essence that had become a part of me. Even though he had departed this world, his spirit would always remain intertwined with mine, providing a modicum of solace.

Watching my grandfather interact with the dragons, I think we both were in our element. A place we could truly call home.

The next thing I knew, strong arms wrapped around me. "For someone who granted us all freedom, you sure are moping around a lot."

I snorted. "I'm sorry, I can't help it."

Shal's arms around me tightened, and I felt a soft kiss on my head. "There is nothing wrong with mourning his loss. He was your best friend, and without him, you wouldn't have been able to do what needed to be done."

I pulled away from Shal's embrace and looked up at him. "I don't know what I would have done without you, either."

He smiled and kissed my forehead again. "You don't need to thank me for anything, I'm just glad we're all safe now because of you. The monster's captive turned goddess and hero to us all. How's that for my next story?"

"I think our kids and grandkids would love it," I said as I kissed him deeply. "Or a story about a girl who fell madly in love with a monster, and they lived happily ever after."

Shal smiled and kissed me back, holding me tight. "I think that's a story we'll have to write together."

Monster's Goddess

Coming 2024-2025

We're so excited to announce that Monster's Goddess will be coming in 2024-2025. It will continue the story of Lila and Shal as she learns how to cope with the loss of Kel and master her newfound power.

About the Author

Luna Jade is a USA Today, bestselling author of sci-fi fantasy romance. She loves to write dangerously sexy stories about antiheroes, monsters, and otherworldly beings worth swooning over. Her books are for dreamers who love to get lost in a world full of magic and mayhem. Luna has created a new world for her readers to enjoy. With every page turned, you'll want to climb into your Kindle and the storyline.

Follow Luna Online

BookBub

Facebook

Beautifully Twisted Newsletter

By joining the Beautifully Twisted Newsletter, you'll get exclusive access to book-themed merch, eBooks, and be the first to know about new releases, pre-orders, and more! You'll also get access to special discounts and promotions. Plus, you'll be part of a community of book lovers who share your passion for reading. So, what are you waiting for? Sign up today!

Here are some of the benefits of joining the Beautifully Twisted Newsletter:

- Exclusive access to book-themed merch, eBooks, and more.
- Be the first to know about new releases, pre-orders, and more.
- E-gift cards, special discounts and promotions.
- BTD Loyalty Program.

Sign up today and start enjoying all the benefits of being a Beautifully Twisted Newsletter subscriber at:

www.beautifullytwistedpublishing.com[1]

Luna Jade also writes under J. P. Uvalle.

BookBub

Facebook

Instagram

TikTok

Other Books and Anthologies

Paranormal & Fantasy Romance

All Things Wild by J. P. Uvalle

The Hidden Souls Trilogy by J. P. Uvalle

Forbitten by J. P. Uvalle

---

1. http://www.beautifullytwistedpublishing.com